Modern Curriculum Press
BEGINNING
TO
READ
Series

CEB'S
Amazing
TAIL

by
David R. Collins
illustrated by Erika W. Kors

Library of Congress Cataloging-in-Publication Data

Collins, David R.
  Ceb's amazing tail.

  Summary: Follows the life of a spider monkey, born with a remarkable tail, and describes his adventures in his native Central American jungle.
    1. Central American spider monkey—Fiction.
[1. Central American spider monkey—Fiction. 2. Monkeys—Fiction] I. Kors, Erika W., ill. II. Title.
PZ10.3.C689Ce 1987   [Fic]   87-10811
ISBN 0-8136-5185-9
ISBN 0-8136-5685-0 (pbk.)

1 2 3 4 5 6 7 8 9   87 88 89 90

MODERN CURRICULUM PRESS

A Division of Simon & Schuster
13900 Prospect Road, Cleveland, Ohio 44136

This is Central America.
Daily rains wash the jungle forests.
A blazing sun beats down.

Treetops spread thick
and full.
Few sunrays slip through.
Yet there is life in the branches.
Among the leaves there is movement.
A troop of spider monkeys is eating
lunch.
Yip and yap, snip and snap.
Tasty nuts are torn from trees.
Wild chatter fills the air.
No monkey will go hungry here.

6

Far below a lone monkey rests.
She squirms and squeals.
Then, a baby spider monkey is born.
Few notice as Ceb enters the world.
His mother likes it that way.
She holds her new baby close.
Ceb drinks his mother's milk.

Ceb is a ball of dark fur.
His face is pink, his nostrils spread
   wide.
His arms are longer than his legs.
Yet his tail is longer than both his arms
   and legs.
Like a thin black rope it curls around.

Ceb holds his mother close.
He clings to her belly and chest.
He wraps his hands tightly.
It is not easy to grip.
Spider monkeys have no thumbs.
Ceb spends his first days sleeping.
Mother tucks him to her front.
Back to the treetops she goes.
Human and animal hunters prowl the
    jungle trails.
It is safe high in the trees.
It is safe with the troop.

9

The troop is Ceb's new family.
There are more females than males.
Most of the females also have babies.
40 monkeys in all, in Ceb's new family.
It makes for loud yipping and yapping
in the trees.

The days pass quickly into weeks.
Mother's milk gives Ceb strength.
Muscles grow in his skinny arms and
    legs.
He still holds his mother close.
A fall from the treetops could kill a
    young spider monkey.
Ceb's eyesight is clear and sharp.
His hearing is not as good.
Yet he can hear the other spider
    monkeys barking.
When a spider monkey gets lost, he
    cries.
It is a high pitched whimper.
All the monkeys cry back.
The lost monkey soon finds his way
    home.

11

Ceb's mother shares the berries and
   nuts she picks.
No longer does Ceb need so much of
   her milk.
He finds a new place to ride.
He climbs on his mother's back.
Ride 'em, spider monkey!

Ceb's hair grows fast.
It becomes long and straggly.
His tail flings out like a whip.
On one side Ceb's tail is furry and soft.
On the other side it is bare skin.
It can feel the dewdrops on the leaves.
It can feel the wind in the breeze.
It can wrap around branches in the
   trees.
It is just like having another hand.

One day Ceb puts his tail
    to use.
He leaves the safety of his
    mother's back.
He leaps forward.
Like hooks his hands grab the next
    branch.
His tail wraps around it too.
Again Ceb jumps, to a far branch.
One hand slips away.
Yet his tail wraps around the branch.
Ceb pulls himself up.
He is ready to jump again.

From branch to branch Ceb swings.
Faster he goes, and faster.
His mother watches nearby.
She knew this day would come.

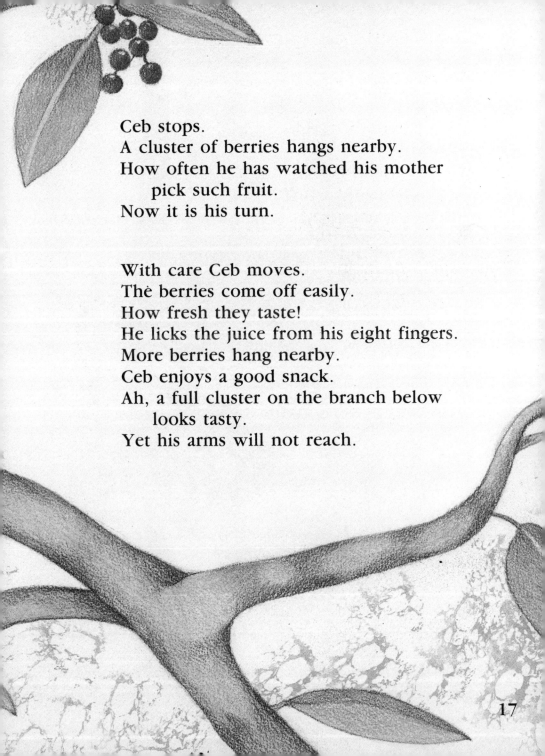

Ceb stops.
A cluster of berries hangs nearby.
How often he has watched his mother
    pick such fruit.
Now it is his turn.

With care Ceb moves.
The berries come off easily.
How fresh they taste!
He licks the juice from his eight fingers.
More berries hang nearby.
Ceb enjoys a good snack.
Ah, a full cluster on the branch below
    looks tasty.
Yet his arms will not reach.

Slowly Ceb wraps his tail around his
     branch.
How strong and firm this tail is.
Ceb leans over.
He lets go with one arm.
Now he releases the other arm.
It works!
The tail becomes a rope.
Ceb uses both hands to eat the berries.
This tail is amazing!

Ceb becomes a scout for the monkey
    troop.
He likes being the first to find a tree
    full of berries.
Nuts and seeds make a good meal too.
Even some flowers are tasty.

Ceb's family spends much time eating
    and sleeping.
Yet grooming takes time too.
Ceb likes being groomed.
Each day his mother smoothes his silky fur.
She nibbles away dry skin and dirt.
She picks off pesty insects.
Then it is Ceb's turn to groom.
He smoothes and cleans his mother's fur.
He does not miss a spot.

20

All the spider monkeys groom.
After grooming, the younger monkeys play.
They chase each other from limb to limb.
There is nothing like tag in the treetops.
Ceb leads the way.
Arm over leg, leg over arm.
His hairless head bobs among the
     branches.
Other young monkeys follow his lead.

Suddenly Ceb stops.
Wild howls fill the air.
They are not the sounds of spider
    monkeys.
Ceb has entered the branches of a troop
    of howler monkeys.

Quickly the spider monkey swings back.
The howler monkeys would not fight.
Yet they make such awful noises.
Ceb wants no part of them.

Ceb wants no part of the ponds that lie
    below either.
Morning dewdrops are fine.
Ceb tastes the tops of the leaves each day.
Spider monkeys care little for water.
Ceb stays off the ground and out of the water.
Life in the treetops is a good life.

Ceb keeps growing.
36 teeth form in his mouth.
Curved and pointed they are, like the
    nails on his fingers.
From head to feet he is 25 inches.
His amazing tail is over 30 inches long.
He weighs 15 pounds.

Ceb remains a child.
He eats, grooms and plays with the
    other young monkeys.
He still stays close to his mother.
Who is his father?
Ceb will never know.
All the males of the troop look after him.
Ceb has many brothers and sisters.

Finally, it is Ceb's turn to seek a mate.
Through the treetops Ceb swings.
Never has he swung so fast.
He walks along branches, his tail
    keeping him steady.
He leads the troop to the finest fruits
    and nuts.
Yes, Ceb is showing off.

There is little need.
Any young female would be
    glad to be his mate.
Ceb makes his choice.
The two spider monkeys go off by
    themselves.

Ceb and his new mate share many meals.
They spend hours grooming.
They swing on vines and branches.

29

Yet Ceb is soon left alone.
His mate goes off by herself.
It is time for her to have a baby.
Ceb is going to become a father.
Again and again this will happen in
        Ceb's life.
He will have many children.
He will stay with the troop all his life.

Finally, when he is thirty, Ceb will tire.
No longer will the arms and legs swing
   through the trees.
Ceb's long tail will curl around his
   body.
The amazing spider monkey will fall
   asleep for the last time.